LiTTLE
BILL
BOOKS FOR
BEGINNING READERS

Hooray for the Dandelion Warriors!

by Bill Cosby

Illustrated by Varnette P. Honeywood

Introduction by Alvin F. Poussaint, M.D.

SCHOLASTIC INC.   Cartwheel ·B·O·O·K·S·®

New York Toronto London Auckland Sydney Mexico City New Delhi Hong Kong

Assistants to art production: Rick Schwab, Nick Naclerio

Library of Congress Cataloging-in-Publication Data

Cosby, Bill, 1937-
  Hooray for the Dandelion Warriors / by Bill Cosby; illustrated by Varnette P. Honeywood.
    p.   cm.— (Little Bill books for beginning readers)
  "Cartwheel books."
  Summary: Little Bill and his teammates are excited to begin baseball practice, but they cannot agree on the team name.
  ISBN 0-590-52191-8 (hardcover) 0-590-52194-2 (pbk)
  [1. Baseball—Fiction. 2. Afro-Americans—Fiction] I. Honeywood, Varnette P., ill.
II. Title. III. Series: Cosby, Bill, 1937-   Little Bill books for beginning readers.
PZ7.C8185Ho   1999
[E]—dc21   99-19026
                                                                            CIP
                                                                             AC
  10 9 8 7 6 5 4 3 2 1   9/9 0/0 01 02 03 04

Printed in the U.S.A. 23
First printing, November 1999

To Ennis,
"Hello, friend,"
B.C.

To the Cosby Family,
Ennis's perseverance against the odds
is an inspiration to us all,
V.P.H.

Dear Parent:

Many young children are eager to play team sports. By age six, boys and girls begin to sharpen their skills—in running and jumping, kicking and throwing—as they grow bigger, stronger, and more coordinated. Traditionally, though, it's the boys who are encouraged to be active in sports, and some little guys assume they're naturally better than girls at games like soccer, basketball, and baseball. Starting in elementary school, girls are teased by some boys, who don't see them as serious athletic competitors.

Although Little Bill's friends (girls as well as boys) are trying out for the baseball team, a gender gap is showing. The boys want the team to have a "tough" name, the Warriors. They make fun of the girls' "wimpy" choice, the Dandelions. And Little Bill is stunned when Simone, who's competing with him for the second-base position, turns out to be a much better hitter and fielder than he is. Embarrassed at being outplayed by a girl, he tries to save face by telling his family that Simone will probably get the second-base slot because she's taller than he is!

His dad, who's clearly from the old school, shames him further by boasting that he never lost a position to a girl in any sport. But his mom reveals the reason: when they were children, the boys wouldn't allow girls to play on their teams. And his great-grandmother reminds him that baseball is a team sport, and a team needs the best players, regardless of gender.

When the coach announces that everybody will initially rotate through all positions, Little Bill is ready to focus on improving his skills no matter what position he gets to play. His feelings are changing for the better as he embraces the wonderful spirit of his mixed-gender team: the Dandelion Warriors.

Alvin F. Poussaint, M.D.
Clinical Professor of Psychiatry,
Harvard Medical School and
Judge Baker Children's Center,
Boston, MA

Chapter One

Hello, friend. My name is Little Bill. This is a story about me and my baseball team.

It was almost time for tryouts. I couldn't wait to join the team! We would get to wear real uniforms and caps, just like the pros. I was trying out for second base. I love second base.

LITTLE **BILL**

Weeks before the tryouts, I practiced hard with my dad. I practiced hitting, catching, throwing, sliding, and running. I could run around the yard so fast. I made sounds of the crowd, cheering and clapping as they watched me.

A lot of my friends were trying out and we had the perfect team all planned. Fuchsia would pitch. Frank would catch. Andrew would play first base. I would play second. José would be on third. Kiku would be in right field. Michael would be in left field. Willie would be in center field.

It was all set. The game would start. We would jog onto the field. And the crowd would cheer and chant our team's name. The question was, what *was* our team's name?

"Let's name ourselves after a flower," said Kiku.

"The Dandelions!" said Fuchsia.

"No way," said Andrew.

"What's wrong with the Dandelions?" Fuchsia asked.

"They're weeds!" said Andrew. He started laughing. So did José. So did I.

"SO?!" said Fuchsia, getting angry.

"So, they're wimpy, how about that?"

"How about, you're wrong," said Kiku. "Dandelions are strong! They can stand up to wind and rain. They can survive anything!"

"Just try to get rid of them. It's impossible!" said Fuchsia, and she gave Kiku a high five.

"Yuck," yelled Michael. "How about the Warriors? Now that's a tough name."

"Yeah, the Warriors," said José, Willie, and I.

"Yuck," said Kiku. "What about the Supremes?"

"No way," said Michael.

"How about the Franks?" said Frank.

It was getting dark, and it was clear we weren't going to pick a name that night. So we all went home. Tryouts were the next day.

Chapter Two

We all got to the tryouts together. When it was my turn to bat, I fouled five balls. Then I got a hit! I ran to first base as fast as I could. Then I made it all the way to third without getting tagged. When I was in the field playing second, I only dropped one pop-fly ball.

Coach White asked me what position I liked to play, and I told him—I always play second base. Just as I was giving Andrew a high five, a very tall girl named Simone came up to the plate. Coach White asked her what position she played and she said second base, too!

It was hard to watch. Simone got one pitch and *WHAM!* She hit the ball, and I think it landed somewhere in the next state.

"Wow," said Coach White. "Let's try that again." The next pitch came and another *WHAM!* And then *BOOM!* The ball hit the wooden fence.

As the players scrambled to get the ball, Simone sped around the bases. With her long legs, she moved so fast, so smoothly that she looked like a superhero about to take off and fly!

I didn't feel so good.

Then Simone went onto the field. From second base, she caught three balls, chased down the kid trying to steal third, and threw out the scoring runner.

"It's all over," I said to Andrew.

"You don't know that until tomorrow when the coach posts the team," Andrew said.

Stupid tomorrow, I thought. Then I walked home.

Back at home, my mom, my dad, and my great-grandmother, Alice the Great, were getting ready for dinner.

"What's the matter, Little Bill?" asked Mom. She can always tell when something's bothering me.

"Nothing," I said.

"How did the tryouts go?" asked Dad.

"It's not fair," I answered. "I always play second base. Now this girl is also trying for second base, and she's much taller than I am!"

My dad took some dishes out of the cabinet and started to set the table. "I never lost a position to a girl in any sport," he said.

"That's because you boys wouldn't let us play," Mom said.

"That's the way it should be," I said. "If girls couldn't be on the team, I'd be playing second base!"

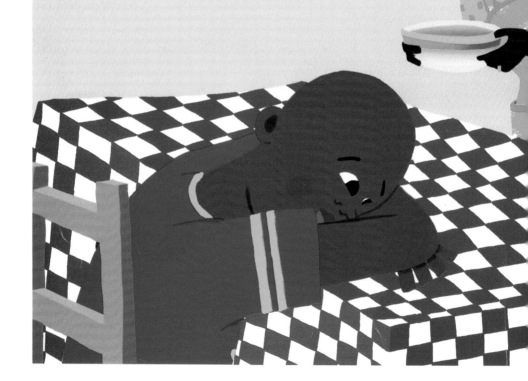

"May I ask you a question?" asked Alice the Great. She looked concerned. "If girls couldn't play, would second base be as good as it's supposed to be on your team?"

"But I want to play second base," I said.

"It seems to me, it's not about this girl. It's about how good a second baseman she is, and how good a second baseman you are."

That night I had a dream that my team was in Game 7 of the World Series. It was a tie game. The bases were loaded. And all we needed was a hit. Simone was up! Hooray! The crowd cheered! We cheered, too.

But all of a sudden, a loud voice said, "NO GIRLS ALLOWED TO PLAY."

The crowd yelled, "BOOOOOOOO!"

We yelled, "BOOOOOOO!"

Simone yelled, "BOOOOOOOOO!"

It wasn't fair! It wasn't fair to our team! Then I woke up.

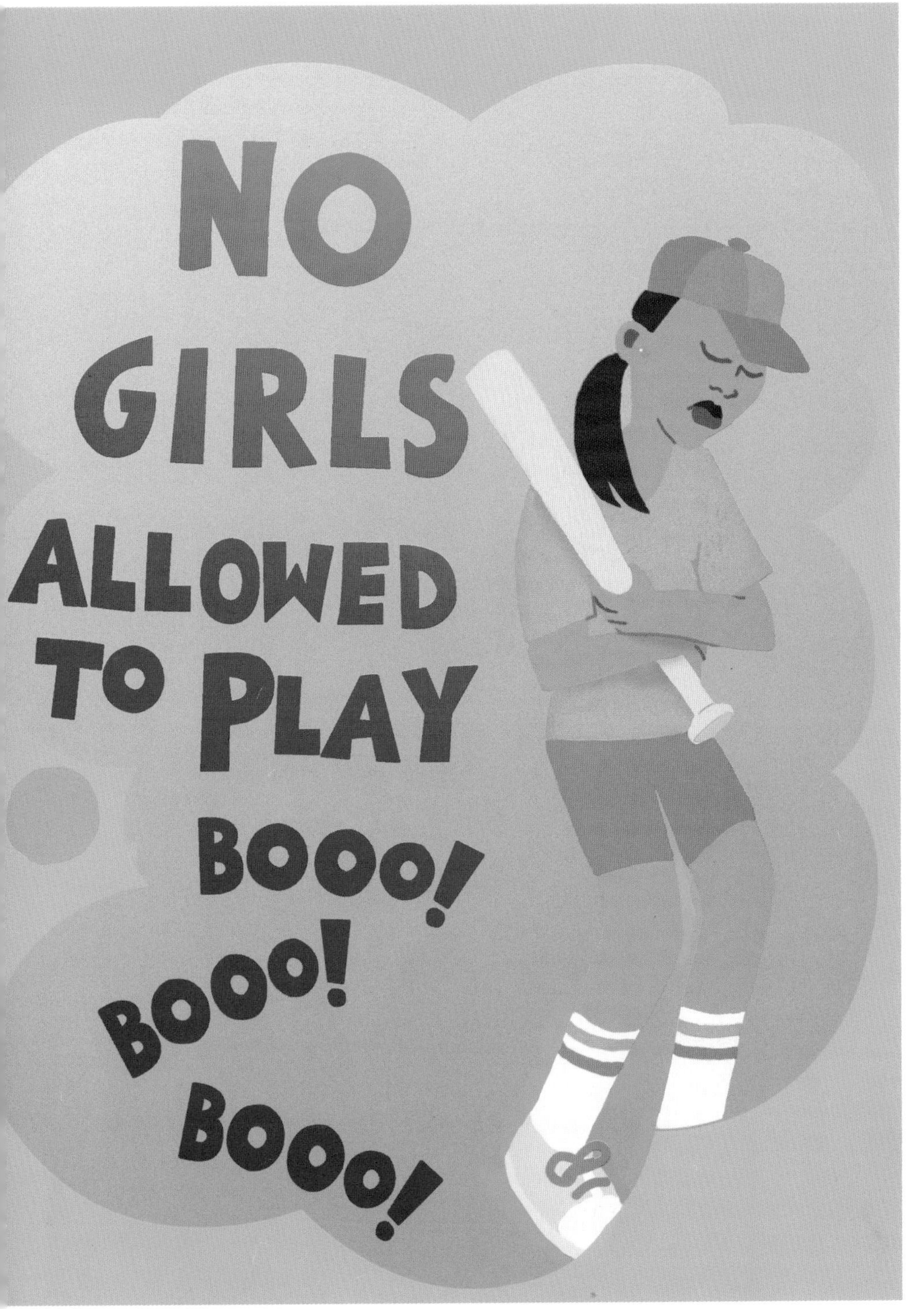
NO GIRLS ALLOWED TO PLAY
BOOO!
BOOO!
BOOO!

Chapter Three

After school the next day, we all ran to the bulletin board where Coach White was posting a list of the new team members. Here is what it said:

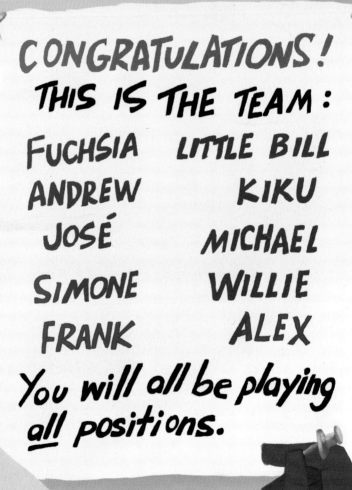

CONGRATULATIONS!
THIS IS THE TEAM:
FUCHSIA   LITTLE BILL
ANDREW   KIKU
JOSÉ   MICHAEL
SIMONE   WILLIE
FRANK   ALEX
You will all be playing all positions.

"What does that mean?" asked Fuchsia.

"Did you forget to give us our positions?" asked Andrew.

"No, I didn't forget," said Coach White. "You will all be playing all positions. A team works best when everyone works together. I'm sure as we practice and work together, you'll all find your places. But for now, everyone plays everything."

"Fuchsia's a great pitcher, but she needs to work on hitting. Frank's a great catcher, but his running needs work. Little Bill's a great runner, but he needs to practice catching."

Hearing I was a great runner made me so happy that I ran all the way home.

The next day we had our first team practice. We all ran the bases, and we practiced throwing and catching, pitching, and hitting. Afterwards, we met with our coach.

"You all did good work today," said Coach White. "It's going to be a great team and a great season. The only thing is, you need to pick a name."

"The Dandelions!" Fuchsia yelled.

"No, the Warriors!" shouted José.

"The Dandelions!" said Kiku and Fuchsia.

"The Warriors!" Michael, Andrew, and I yelled together.

"The Franks!" yelled Frank.

The Warriors! The Dandelions! Warriors! Dandelions! Warriors! Everyone yelled.

"Terrific name!" shouted Coach White. Everyone stopped yelling.

"Which name?" asked Simone.

"Both of them," said Coach White. "The Dandelion Warriors! There's no other team quite like it!"

"The Dandelion Warriors and Frank! Yes!" joked Frank.

"The Dandelion Warriors," said Simone. "I like that. It's weird, but cool."

"Me too," said Michael.

"Me three," said José.

"Me four," said Frank.

The coach put his hand out and said, "Let's hear it for the Dandelion Warriors!" We all piled our hands on top of his, until there was a huge pile of hands. Then we all yelled, "GO DANDELION WARRIORS!" and threw our hands up in the air.

That night, I climbed into bed with my baseball cap and my glove. Soon we would get our real uniforms and caps. Maybe I would play second base. Maybe I would play somewhere else. It didn't matter as long as I had a chance to play, and as long as I had a chance to be a better player.

Whatever happened, I was a part of the Dandelion Warriors. There was no other name like it. And there was no other team like it. A few minutes later, I was dreaming we had won the World Series.

HOWARD L. BINGHAM

HOWARD L. BINGHAM

Bill Cosby is one of America's best-loved storytellers, known for his work as a comedian, actor, and producer. His books for adults include *Fatherhood*, *Time Flies*, *Love and Marriage*, and *Childhood*. Mr. Cosby holds a doctoral degree in education from the University of Massachusetts.

Varnette P. Honeywood, a graduate of Spelman College and the University of Southern California, is a Los Angeles-based fine artist. Her work is included in many collections throughout the United States and Africa and has appeared on adult trade book jackets and in other books in the Little Bill series.

Books in the LITTLE BILL series:

The Best Way to Play
None of the parents will buy the new *Space Explorers* video game. How can Little Bill and his friends have fun without it?

The Day I Was Rich
Little Bill has found a giant diamond and now he's the richest boy in the world. How will he and his friends spend all that money?

Hooray for the Dandelion Warriors!
It's the boys against the girls. But wait! Everybody is supposed to be on the same team!

The Meanest Thing to Say
All the kids are playing a new game. You have to be mean to win it. Can Little Bill be a winner...and be nice, too?

Money Troubles
Funny things happen when Little Bill tries to earn some money.

My Big Lie
Little Bill's tiny fib grew and grew and GREW into a BIG lie. And now Little Bill is in BIG trouble.

One Dark and Scary Night
Little Bill can't fall asleep! There's something in his closet that might try to get him.

Shipwreck Saturday
All by himself, Little Bill built a boat out of sticks and a piece of wood. The older boys say that his boat won't float. He'll show them!

Super-Fine Valentine
Little Bill's friends are teasing him! They say he's *in love*! Will he get them to stop?

The Treasure Hunt
Little Bill searches his room for his best treasure. What he finds is a great big surprise!

The Worst Day of My Life
On the worst day of his life, Little Bill shows his parents how much he loves them. And he changes a bad day into a good one!